Scholastic Children's Books,
Euston House, 24 Eversholt Street,
London NW1 1DB, UK

A division of Scholastic Ltd
London ~ New York ~ Toronto ~ Sydney ~ Auckland
Mexico City ~ New Delhi ~ Hong Kong

Published in the UK by Scholastic Ltd, 2019

TRADE EDITION ISBN 978 1407 19830 9
SCHOLASTIC CLUBS AND FAIRS EDITION ISBN 978 1407 19938 2

Printed and bound in Italy by L.E.G.O S.p.A

2 4 6 8 10 9 7 5 3 1

www.scholastic.co.uk

It was Jess's birthday. She was having a party and all the guests had to bring a pet with them. Her own pet was Waffle, who was a very special dog indeed.

Gramps had brought two more pups to the party. "Say hello to Muckypups and Thor," he said. "I'm dog-sitting them for the day."

"Welcome to my 'Bring a Pet Party'!" Jess greeted the pups.

"Woof!" barked Waffle.

Gramps gave Jess her birthday present to unwrap. It was a knitted jumper with a picture of Waffle on the front!

"It's me!" woofed Waffle, wagging his tail.

"I love it!" smiled Jess, putting on the jumper. "Thank you, Dad."

"Happy birthday!" Waffle barked.

There were lots of amazing pets at the party. Anaya and AJ had brought their pet gecko, Leo, and their two goldfish, Dipper and Dabber.

Evie decorated Leo's tank with some spotty bunting. It was just right for a spotty gecko!

Then, Doug fetched some food for the fish.

Soon, it was time for Waffle's big birthday performance. Simon had been teaching him some special tricks.

First, Waffle chased his tail in a circle.

"Good boy!" smiled Simon, as everybody clapped and cheered.

Waffle's next trick was to jump through a hoop.

"Well done, Waffle!" Gramps cheered.

Waffle loved showing off his clever tricks!

Just then, the doorbell rang. Mr Meagre had arrived with his pet parrot, Pickles.

"Sorry we're late," Mr Meagre said to Jess. "Have we missed all the sandwiches and cake?"

"Pieces of cake! Pieces of cake!" squawked Pickles.

"No," smiled Jess. "Follow me upstairs to all the party food."

Waffle had just finished his last trick as Mr Meagre and Pickles appeared.

"The party entertainment was provided by Waffle the Wonder Dog," said Simon. "Take a bow, Waffle!"

But Pickles wanted to see Waffle's tricks, too. "More! More! More!" chirped the parrot.

"I think Waffle has finished his tricks for today," Simon told Pickles.

"Waffle, say hello to Pickles. He loves performing, too," said Mr Meagre. He put Pickles' cage down on the floor, next to Waffle.

"Happy birthday to you!" Pickles squawked. "I'm the star, not you!" he chirped, and everyone giggled.

"Pickles is funny, isn't he, Mum?" Evie said to Jess.

"He is..." Jess agreed. "He's a star!"

"Can you say a joke, Pickles?" Mr Meagre asked his parrot.

"A joke! A joke! A joke!" Pickles repeated. The noisy parrot wouldn't stop squawking!

Waffle whispered an idea to Gramps. Then Gramps took off his jacket and used it to cover Pickles' cage.

"Bye bye, Pickles!" woofed Waffle. And everyone laughed.

"Sorry, Pickles," said Mr Meagre, removing the jacket. "But that was funny!"

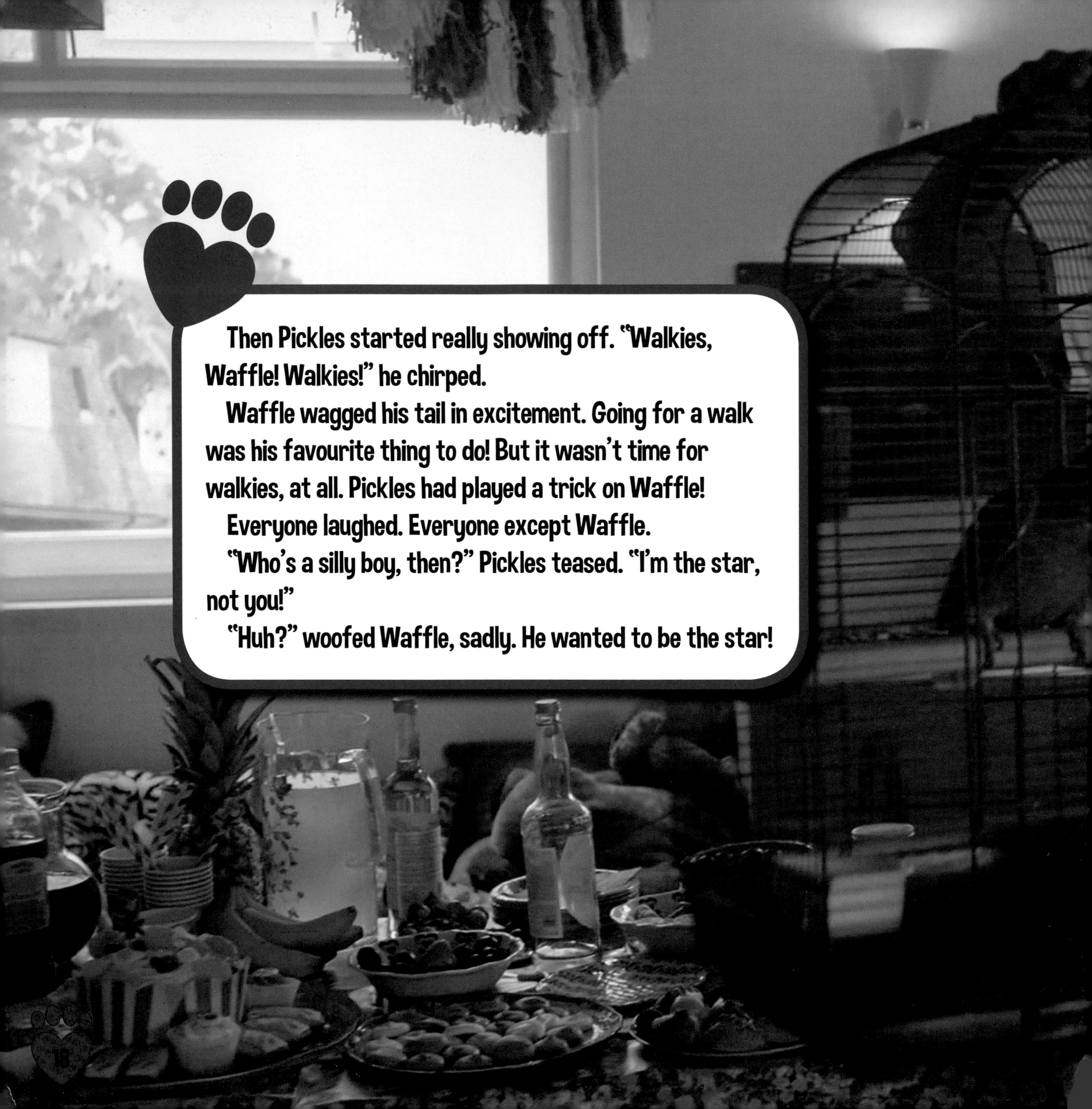

Then Pickles started really showing off. "Walkies, Waffle! Walkies!" he chirped.

Waffle wagged his tail in excitement. Going for a walk was his favourite thing to do! But it wasn't time for walkies, at all. Pickles had played a trick on Waffle!

Everyone laughed. Everyone except Waffle.

"Who's a silly boy, then?" Pickles teased. "I'm the star, not you!"

"Huh?" woofed Waffle, sadly. He wanted to be the star!

Next, Waffle had an idea that would make him top dog. He scampered downstairs and found Simon's guitar.

Doug and Simon followed Waffle into the kitchen.

"I need you to play your guitar upstairs, Dad," Waffle woofed.

Simon was puzzled. "OK, Waffle," he said.

A few minutes later, Waffle was ready to perform his best trick ever.

"Welcome back the star of the party ... Waffle!" said Simon grandly. Everyone clapped and cheered. Simon picked up his guitar and began to sing, "Oh, Waffle..."

"Oh, Waffle, I'm Waffle," Waffle joined in. "Leaping around like a..."

"Frog?" sang Simon, surprised. No one had ever heard Waffle sing before!

"Wow!" gasped Doug. "Waffle can sing!"

"Waffle, you ARE the star!" added Evie, when Waffle had finished his song.

Even Pickles was proud. "Who's a clever doggy? Who's a clever doggy?" the parrot squawked.

The party celebrations continued. This time, everyone joined in with Waffle's song, dancing and singing until it was time to go home.

"Waffle doggy!
Waffle doggy!
You're such a clever dog,
You're such a clever dog,
you are..."

And from that day on, it was hard to get Waffle to stop singing! Waffle certainly was a very special dog.